CUENTO
DE LUZ

To my two chicks Alvaro and Jorge, who open my eyes to the joy of the moment.
- Marta Zafrilla -

Water and tear resistant
Produced without water, without trees and without bleach
Saves 50% of energy compared to normal paper

Chirpy Charlie's Teeth
Text © 2017 Marta Zafrilla
Illustrations © 2017 Sonja Wimmer
This edition © 2017 Cuento de Luz SL
Calle Claveles, 10 | Urb. Monteclaro | Pozuelo de Alarcón | 28223 | Madrid | Spain
www.cuentodeluz.com
Title in Spanish: Los dientes de Trino Rojo
English translation by Jon Brokenbrow
Printed in PRC by Shanghai Chenxi Printing Co., Ltd. February 2017, print number 1663-3
ISBN: 978-84-16733-30-9

CHIRPY CHARLIE'S TEETH

Marta Zafrilla

Sonja Wimmer

"Julie, brush your teeth, or you'll need a filling!" yelled Julie's mom.

Well, I'm a little bird who looks after his health, and all this business about getting a filling must be horrible, because she talks about it every day. There's no way I'm going to have one of those things in my teeth.

I carefully watched Julie
brushing her teeth, but there's
one thing I can't quite work out.
How do birds brush their teeth?

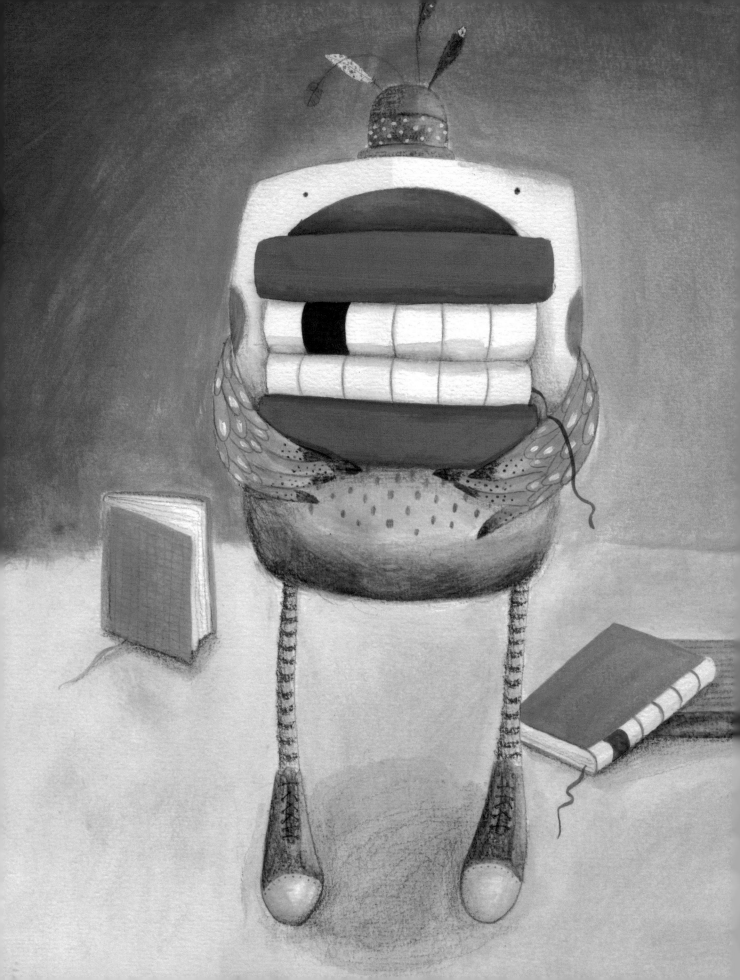

I looked it up in the encyclopedia, but I couldn't find anything. I don't want problems with my teeth because I don't look after them properly! Just like Julie's mom says, teeth are for your whole life. I searched and searched, but there was nothing in the books, or on the Internet.

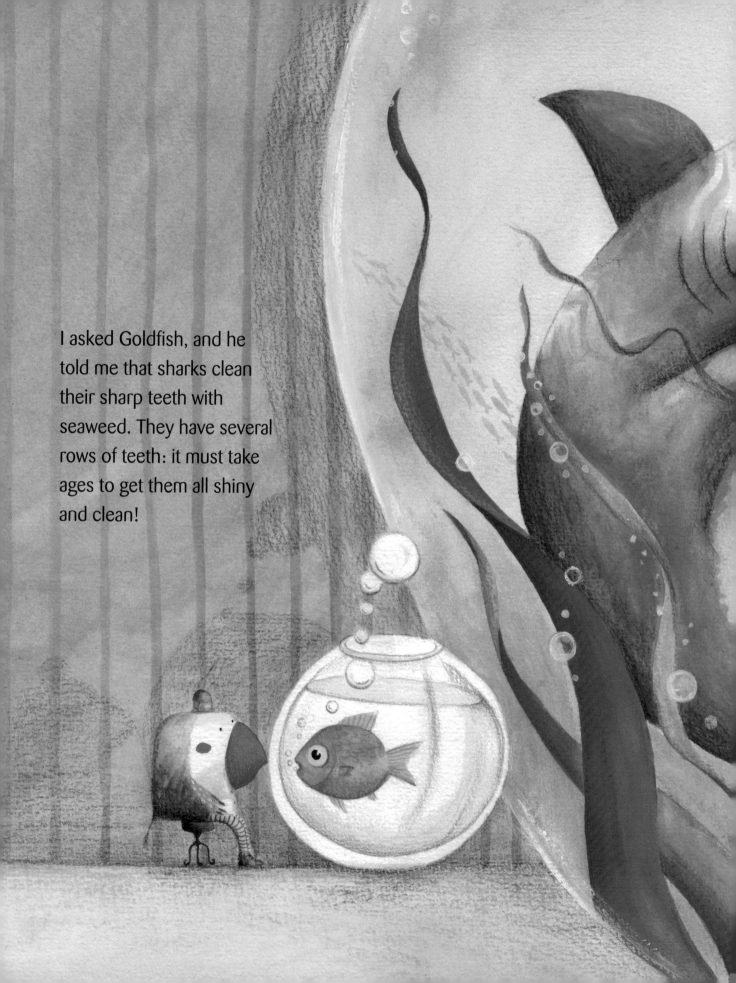

I asked Goldfish, and he told me that sharks clean their sharp teeth with seaweed. They have several rows of teeth: it must take ages to get them all shiny and clean!

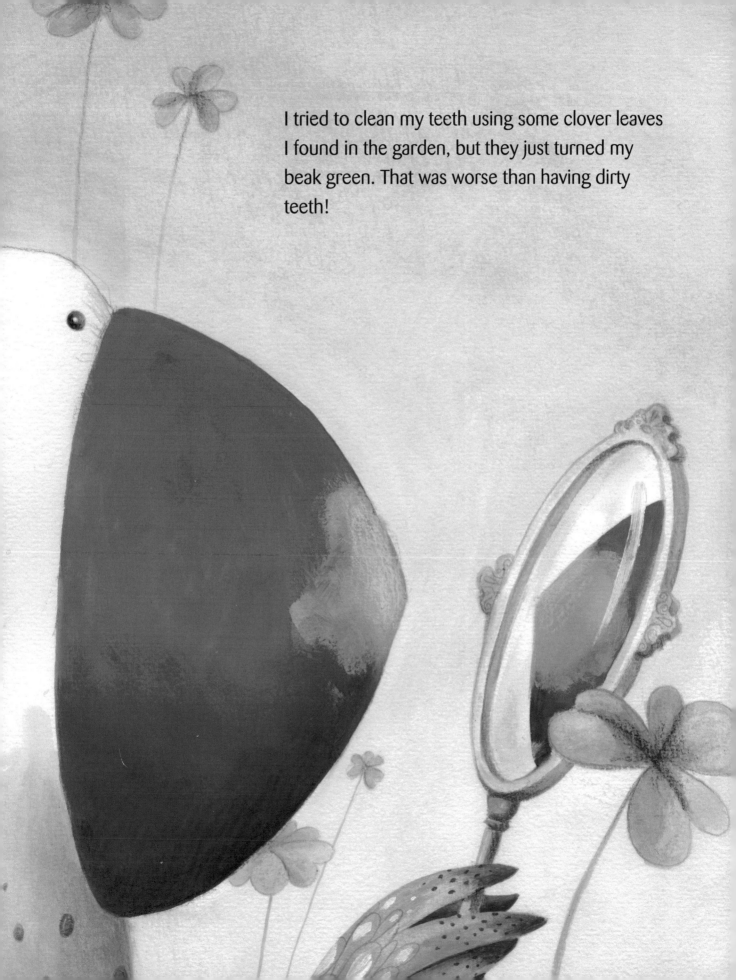

I tried to clean my teeth using some clover leaves I found in the garden, but they just turned my beak green. That was worse than having dirty teeth!

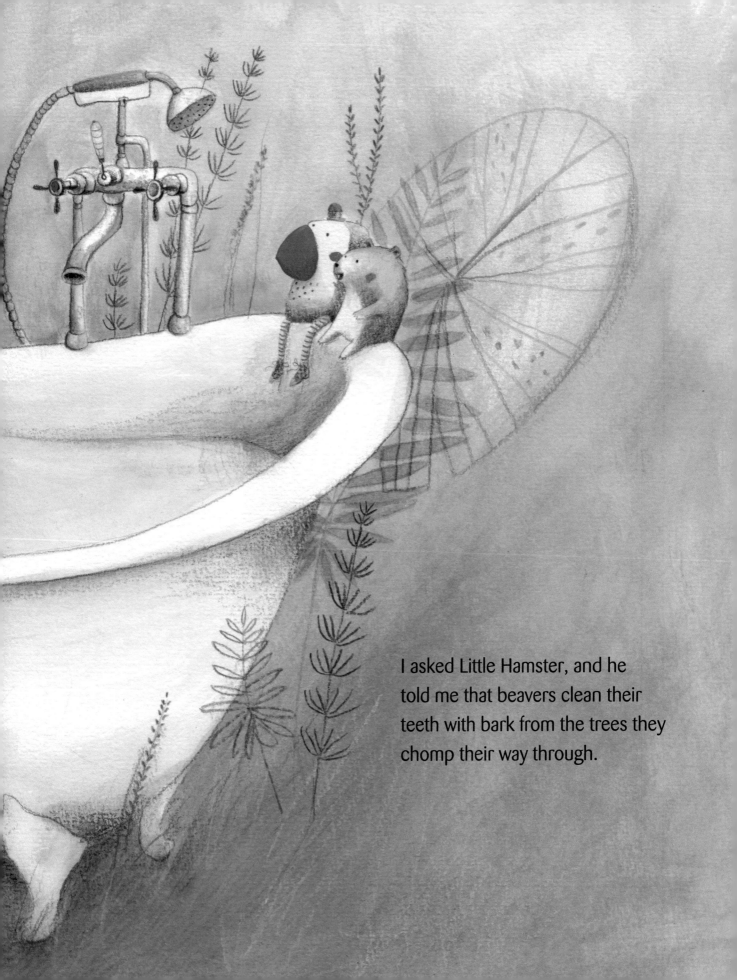

I asked Little Hamster, and he told me that beavers clean their teeth with bark from the trees they chomp their way through.

I decided to try and clean my teeth against one of the legs of the kitchen table, but all that happened was Julie's mom yelled at me, and I ended up with a really sore beak.

When I asked Ant about it, she told me that grasshoppers clean their saw-edged teeth by chopping down flowers.

So I thought I'd try it out with some lovely orchids that were in the front room. All I managed to do was to tip over the pot. Julie's dad stomped around with a confused look on his face, trying to work out what on earth had happened. Uh-oh!

Finally, I decided to try out a toothbrush, just for myself, to 'fight off the fillings' like Julie says every time she cleans her teeth. So I flapped into the bathroom, and tried to pick one up out of the glass. But my beak isn't very good at grabbing things, and … crash! What a mess!

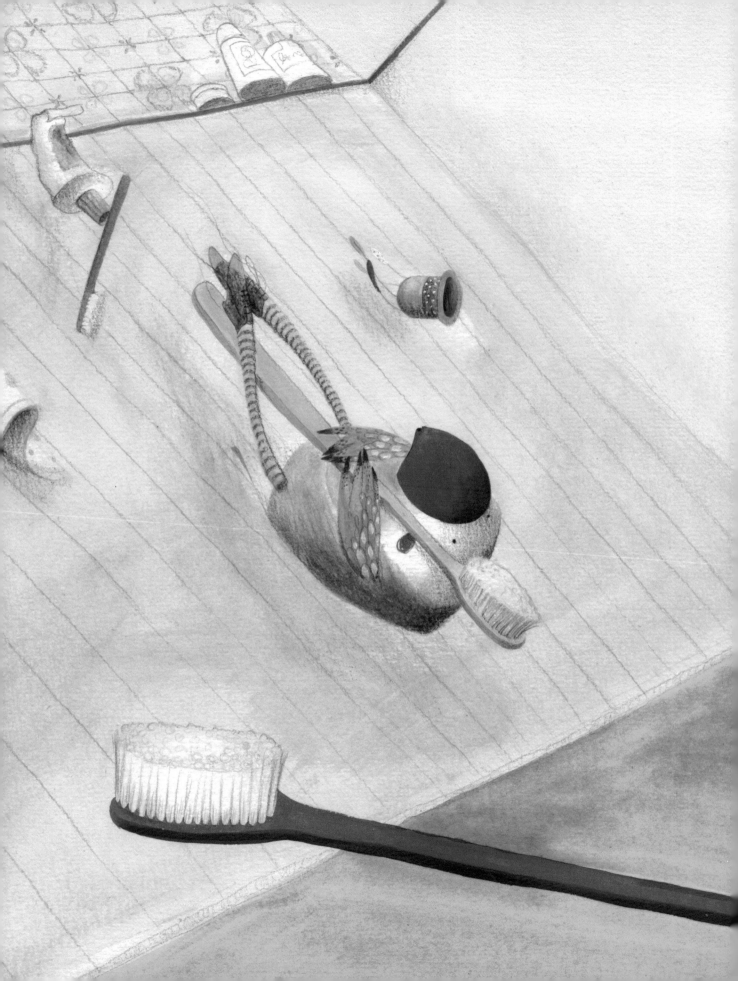

Julie ran into the bathroom, wondering what all the noise was about. "What are you up to, Charlie? Do you want to brush your teeth?" I looked up at her with relief, glad that she had finally worked out what I wanted. "Chirpy Charlie, you can't brush your teeth," she said, in a very serious voice. "You don't have any!"

What do you mean,
I don't have any teeth?

That's impossible!

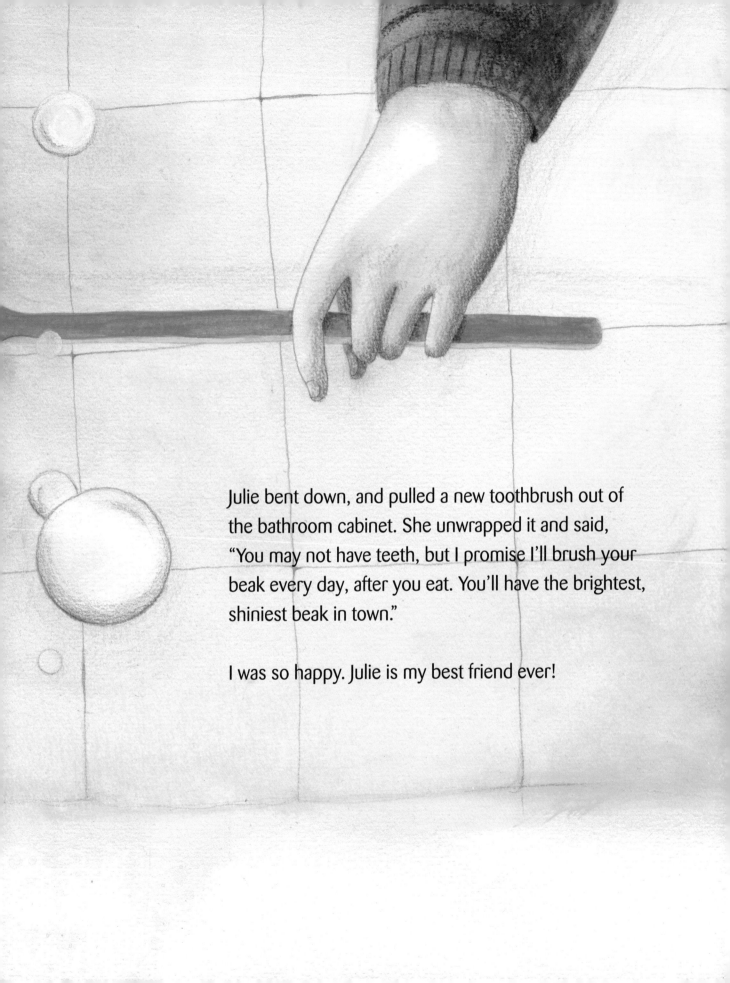

Julie bent down, and pulled a new toothbrush out of the bathroom cabinet. She unwrapped it and said, "You may not have teeth, but I promise I'll brush your beak every day, after you eat. You'll have the brightest, shiniest beak in town."

I was so happy. Julie is my best friend ever!